MEET BIG FOOT

By Michelle H. Nagler
Illustrated by Duendes del Sur
Hello Reader — Level 1

ISBN 0-439-31848-3

Copyright © 2002 by Hanna-Barbera.
SCOOBY-DOO and all related characters and elements are trademarks of and © Hanna-Barbera.
CARTOON NETWORK and logo are trademarks of and © Cartoon Network.
(s02)
All rights reserved. Published by Scholastic Inc.
SCHOLASTIC, HELLO READER, and associated logos are trademarks and/or registered trademarks of Scholastic Inc.

Designed by Maria Stasavage
Printed in China

and the gang were excited.

They were staying in a

in the .

"There's a in back," said

 .

 wanted to swim in the

 .

"After we unpack the ,"

said .

and took suitcases

out of the  .

 took .

" , let's unpack the of

food," said  . "I'm hungry."

But in the kitchen, and

 heard scary noises.

"What's that?" asked 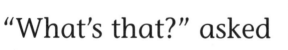 .

"Probably some other campers

in the ," said .

and went swimming.

 , , and  tried

to catch  with .

"Got one!" yelled .

They took the big into the

kitchen.

 and were all alone.

"Look!" said , pointing across

the .

"A !"

and ran back to the

 .

" !" yelled .

 used his to show how

big the was.

But when 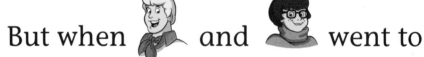 and went to

look, it was gone.

"It must have been a ," said

 .

and cooked the .

", will you and go get

some  for the ?"

asked .

"Ro ray!" barked .

"There's a in the !"

said .

"Would you do it for two ?"

asked .

"Ro kay!" barked .

and went into the

 .

 found some .

"Great!" said . "Let's take

them for the ."

Then found some  .

"Yikes!" said  . "Maybe the

 left these  ! Let's get

out of here!"

But on the way back to the , tripped.

And his  landed in . . .

. . . deep, wide 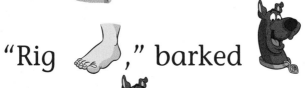!

"These are too big for a ,"

said .

"Rig ," barked .

"Uh-oh, , you're right —

Big !" said . "Run!"

 and showed ,

, and the .

"These are very big.

And there are weird all

over," said .

"Looks like a mystery!" said

. "Let's look for clues."

, , and looked for

clues near the .

and searched the .

"Zoinks!" said . "This is where we saw Big !"

They found of and .

"Big must like and , , just like us!" said .

Suddenly, and  heard a noise in the .

The 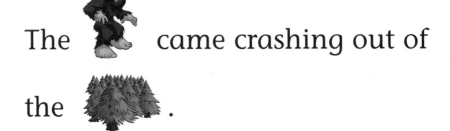 came crashing out of the 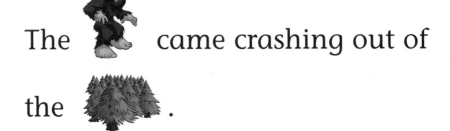 .

"He must be mad at us for eating his food!" said 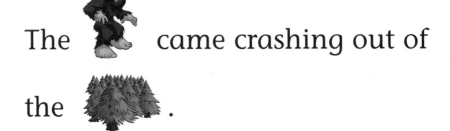 .

But right behind Big 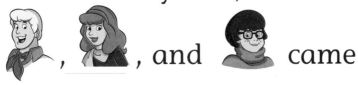 was a big .

And a man yelled, "Cut!"

 , , and came running.

"What happened?" asked .

The man with the said,

"We're making a Big

movie."

"That explains the !"

said .

"And the ?"said .

The man nodded. "Do you know

anyone who wants to be in a

movie?"

 barked. "Scooby-Dooby-Doo!"

Did you spot all the picture clues in this Scooby-Doo mystery?

Each picture clue is on a flash card. Ask a grown-up to cut out the flash cards. Then try reading the words on the back of the cards. The pictures will be your clue.

Reading is fun with Scooby-Doo!

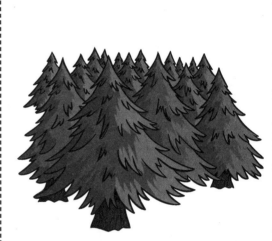

cabin	Shaggy
forest	Scooby
Daphne	lake

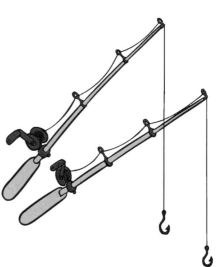

Fred	van
fishing poles	Velma
monster	bags

paws	fish
fire	bear
Scooby Snacks	sticks

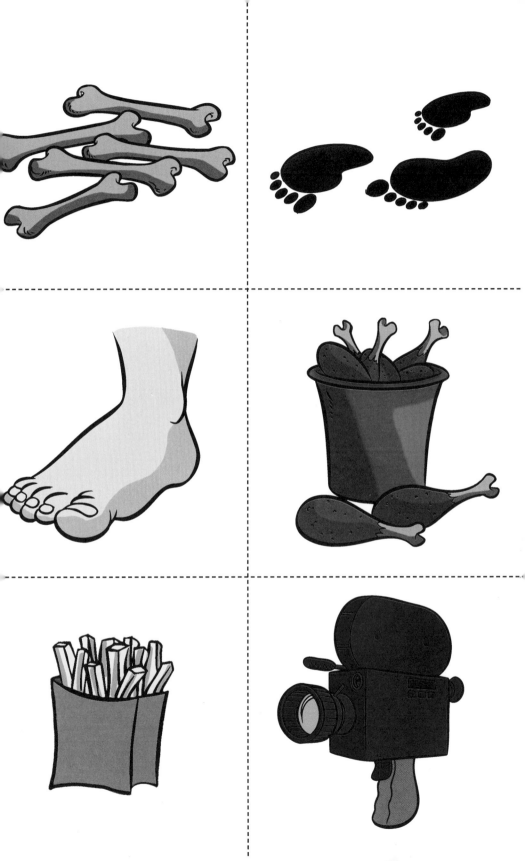

footprints	bones
chicken	foot
camera	fries